Char Siu Bao Boy

Sandra S. Yamate

Illustrations by Carolina Yao

Polychrome Publishing Corporation
Chicago, Illinois

Library of Congress Cataloging-in-Publication Data

Yamate, Sandra S.
Char Siu Bao Boy / by Sandra S. Yamate;
illustrated by Carolina Yao
              p.   cm.

Summary: After being ridiculed by the others at school,
Charlie abandons his favorite Chinese food, char siu bao,
and tries to eat more "normal" things, but then finds a
way to convert his friends to the tasty dish.

ISBN 1-879965-19-4
[1. Food—Fiction. 2. Chinese Americans—Fiction.]

I. Yao, Carolina, ill.
II. Title.

PZ7.Y1919 Ch 2000
[E]—dc21
99-088850

This is a new book, written and illustrated
especially for Polychrome Books
First Edition, Fall, 2000

Designed, produced and published by
Polychrome Publishing Corporation
4509 North Francisco Avenue
Chicago, Illinois 60625-3808
(773) 478-4455 Fax: (773) 478-0786
website: http://home.earthlink.net/~polypub/

Editorial Director: Sandra S. Yamate
Production Coordinator: Brian M. Witkowski
Art Director: Jeanne Wang

Printed in China
By O.G. Printing Productions Ltd.
10 9 8 7 6 5 4 3 2 1

ISBN 1-879965-19-4

Charlie liked char siu bao.

He liked it better than candy.
He liked it better than cookies.
He liked it better than pizza.
It was his FAVORITE food.

Charlie liked char siu bao steamed.
He liked it baked. He even liked it COLD.

Sometimes, Charlie helped Grandmother make char siu bao. He helped her bake the bright red barbecued pork that was the char siu.

He helped her roll the fluffy dough that would be wrapped around the char siu.

He helped her shape them into nice round balls.

Best of all, Charlie helped sample
each batch of char siu bao...
    ...just to make sure it tasted DELICIOUS!

Every day when Charlie went
to school, he carried his lunch.

SCHOOL BUS

And every day for lunch
he brought char siu bao.

All of the other boys and girls made
faces when Charlie ate his char siu bao.

"UGH!" said the boys.

"YECH!" said the girls.

"Why can't you eat a sandwich like everyone else?" asked his best friend Mike.

"Char siu bao is like a sandwich," explained Charlie. "It's a Chinese sandwich."

It didn't matter. All the other boys and girls thought char siu bao looked TERRIBLE.

So, Charlie tried to eat other things for lunch.

One day he brought a peanut butter sandwich. Another day he brought a hot dog. Still another day he brought a ham sandwich, and then egg salad. Before long, he had tried tuna salad, turkey, and even salami sandwiches.

"Aren't they good?"
asked the other boys and girls.

Charlie didn't say anything.
He missed his delicious char siu bao.

Then one day Charlie had an idea.

He whispered his idea to Grandmother.
She smiled and nodded.

The next day at lunchtime each boy and girl found a char siu bao in front of them.

"I've tried to eat sandwiches that you like," said Charlie. "Now it's your turn to try the char siu bao that I like. It's not fair for you to make faces at it until you've tried it."

The boys and girls looked at each other. It was true. None of them had ever tried char siu bao before.

They looked at the char siu bao.

Some SNIFFED at it.

Some POKED at it.

Charlie wondered if anyone would try a piece of char siu bao.

Finally, his best friend Mike
looked at him and sighed.

Mike picked up the char siu bao. He took a deep breath. Everyone was silent, watching Mike. Mike bit into the char siu bao. He chewed, he swallowed...

...and he smiled.

"HEY, this is GOOD!" exclaimed Mike.

The other boys and girls each picked up their char siu bao. Some took BIG bites. Some took little bites.

Before long, EVERYONE was eating char siu bao!

"This char siu bao IS delicious!
We're glad we tried it!" they said.
"Thank you, Charlie."

Charlie smiled. "You're welcome," he said.
"I'm happy to share my favorite food
with all my friends."

Now, Charlie still brings
char siu bao for lunch every day.

But he also brings extras...

...to share with all his friends.

The End

Grandmother's Char Siu Bao

Char Siu

1 pound lean pork
2 tablespoons sugar
2 tablespoons red bean curd (nam yoy)
1 tablespoon soy sauce
1 tablespoon sherry
1/2 teaspoon salt
1/4 teaspoon Chinese five spice powder (heong liu fun)
1/4 teaspoon Chinese red food coloring (hoong soi)

Cut pork into approximately 1" x 2" x 6" pieces.

Combine remaining ingredients. Marinate pork in the mixture for at least one hour, preferably three hours. Place the pork pieces in a shallow roasting pan and roast at 375 degrees for 1 hour. Let cool.

Chop into bite size or somewhat smaller pieces (about 1/2 inch to 1/4 inch pieces).

Char Siu Bao Dough

1 package yeast
8 cups flour
1 cup warm (not hot) water
with 2 teaspoons sugar dissolved in it
1/2 cup sugaar
1/3 cup oil
1 teaspoon salt

Proof the yeast for one hour in the warm sugar water. Mix with remaining ingredients to form the dough. Knead the dough until smooth and elastic. Place dough in a greased bowl and cover with a kitchen towel. Let the dough rise in a warm place, for about two hours, or until its bulk has tripled. Remove dough from the bowl and punch down; knead again until smooth and elastic. Roll the dough into a long roll and divide it into approximately two dozen rounds. Flatten each round and place a spoonful of the char siu in the center. Wrap the dough around the filling to make a ball. Place each ball seam-side down on a small square of wax paper. Allow the balls to rise for one hour then steam for 12-15 minutes.

Acknowledgements

Polychrome Publishing appreciates the support, help, and encouragement received from Theodora B. Chann; Hannah Chow; Michael and Kay Janis; Jeanne Wang; Mitchell and Laura Witkowski; and George and Vicki Yamate. Without them, this book would not have been possible.

About Polychrome Publishing

Founded in 1990, Polychrome Publishing Corporation is an independent press located in Chicago, Illinois, producing children's books for a multicultural market. Polychrome books introduce characters and illustrate situations with which children of all colors can identify. They are designed to promote racial, ethnic, cultural, and religious tolerance and understanding. We live in a multicultural world. We at Polychrome Publishing believe that our children need a balanced multicultural education if they are to thrive in that world. Polychrome books can help create that balance.